OTHER YEARLING BOOKS BY GARY PAULSEN YOU WILL ENJOY

MR. TUCKET

CALL ME FRANCIS TUCKET

TUCKET'S RIDE

TUCKET'S GOLD

LAWN BOY

MUDSHARK

TUCKET'S HOME

★

GARY PAULSEN

A YEARLING BOOK

Copyright © 2000 by Gary Paulsen
Map copyright © 1994 by Virginia Norey

All rights reserved. Published in the United States by Yearling, an imprint of Random House Children's Books, a division of Random House, Inc., New York. Originally published in hardcover in the United States by Delacorte Press, an imprint of Random House Children's Books, a division of Random House, Inc., New York, in 2000.

Yearling and the jumping horse design are registered trademarks of Random House, Inc.

Visit us on the Web! www.randomhouse.com/kids

Educators and librarians, for a variety of teaching tools, visit us at www.randomhouse.com/teachers

Library of Congress Cataloging-in-Publication Data is available upon request.

ISBN 978-0-440-41558-9 (pbk.)

Printed in the United States of America

19 18 17 16 15 14 13 12 11

Random House Children's Books supports the First Amendment and celebrates the right to read.

TUCKET'S HOME

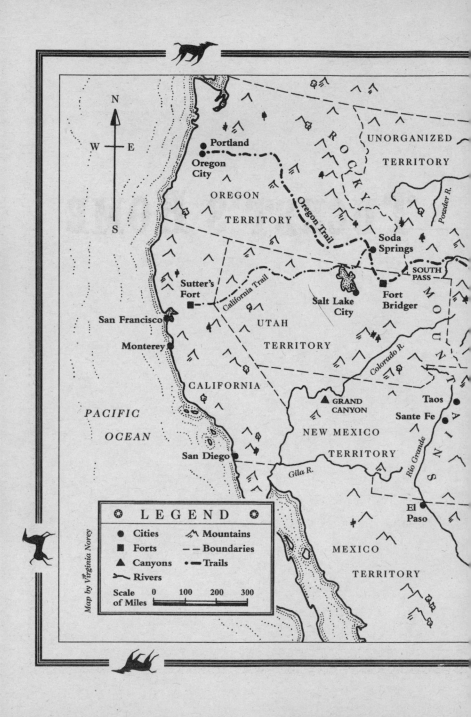

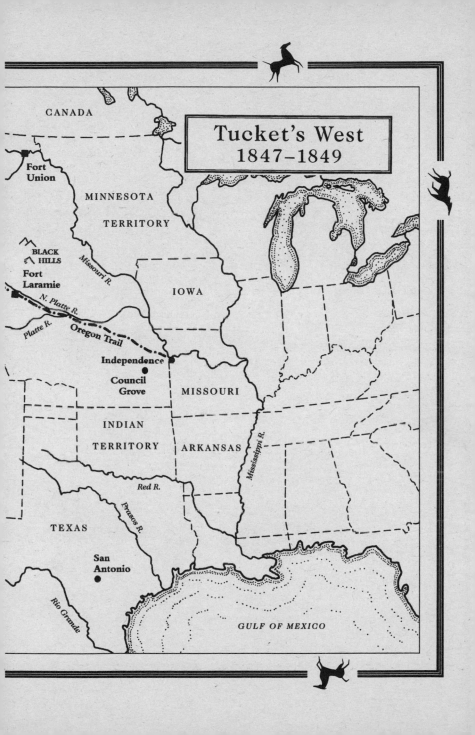

Tucket's West
1847–1849

CANADA

Fort
Union

MINNESOTA

TERRITORY

BLACK
HILLS

Fort
Laramie

Missouri R.

N. Platte R.

Platte R.

Oregon Trail

IOWA

Independence

Council
Grove

MISSOURI

INDIAN

TERRITORY

ARKANSAS

Mississippi R.

Red R.

Brazos R.

TEXAS

San
Antonio

Rio Grande

GULF OF MEXICO

Chapter One

Francis Tucket lay quietly, the sun warming his back, and watched a small herd of buffalo below him in a depression on the prairie. There were only fifteen or twenty of them, mostly cows with some yearling calves. Two young bulls were sparring, tearing up the dirt and raising dust in great clouds.

He turned to look behind him, where ten-year-old Lottie watched their horses graze. Her little brother, Billy, crouched beside her, making an arrow. Francis looked down at the buffalo. The sun was gentle on his back, the dust from the fight was drifting away on a soft breeze, and as Francis lay watching, he let his mind wander back over the trip since he and Lottie and Billy had left the Pueblo Indian village.

They'd stayed there a month so that Francis could recover from a snakebite. With the help of some of the Indians, Lottie had pulled him through, while Billy had learned to hunt and shoot a bow and arrow with amazing skill. The village had been a peaceful place.

Now Francis shifted and scanned the horizon. Even in a quiet moment like this one, you had to be alert, ready for anything. They'd all learned that the hard way.

Francis Tucket had been separated from his family more than a year before, on his fourteenth birthday, when Pawnees kidnapped him from a wagon train. Jason Grimes, a one-armed mountain man, had helped him escape and taught him to survive. After they parted, Francis had found Lottie and Billy alone on the prairie, their father dead of cholera. They'd been members of a wagon train that abandoned them when their father became sick, for fear that he would infect others in the train. So the three had stuck together and headed west to the Oregon Trail to find Francis's family.

Lottie had proved to be the best organizer and camper Francis had ever seen, and Billy, now just shy of eight, had become a hunting and scouting machine of the first order. They'd been through some hair-raising adventures: Kidnapped by the Comanchero outlaw band. Storms. Snakebite. Ambushed by the murderous thieves Courtweiler and Dubs. The three had shared plenty, good and bad, and now they shared a secret—the ancient Spanish silver and gold they carried on the packhorse. When they were being chased by the Comancheros Billy had stumbled upon the grave of a Spanish conquistador, buried with his armor, sword and plunder of centuries ago. Of course, gold and silver meant nothing out here in the wilderness. But someday, someday they'd find Francis's family and civilization, though they still had five hundred miles of rough country to cover alone.

Francis had feared there would be problems on this part of their journey, but it had turned out to be nothing more than a camping trip in a country so beautiful that Francis often had trouble believing it was real.

They had started in partial desert, country covered in mesquite and piñons, but it quickly gave way to mountains. Spring had come early and had stayed. Thick, green grass kept the horses well fed and happy; streams ran full of cold water and trout. Billy caught the fish easily, using a skill he'd learned from the Pueblos that required only a bit of line braided from horsehair, taken from the ponies' tails, and a bent and sharpened piece of wire.

Francis had no trouble getting deer with his rifle, and Billy supplemented the venison and trout diet with rabbit and turkey and grouse he shot with his bow. Within a week they were all getting fat, and the packhorse nearly staggered with extra meat as they rode through grassy mountain meadows amid high mountain peaks still covered with snow.

But they hadn't seen any buffalo until they'd come to this rise and seen below them the small herd with the fighting bulls.

"Honestly, Francis, I don't see why we need more meat." Lottie had crawled up alongside him. Billy, his arrow finished, was a hundred yards back, below the ridge, adjusting the makeshift packs on the horses. "We have so much now we can't carry it all."

"Not so loud—if the wind shifts they'll hear us and run," Francis whispered. "The reason is that we don't have *buffalo* meat. Besides that, they're fat and we need the grease for our moccasins and leather and my rifle. So we're going to shoot a buffalo, all right?"

She nodded and became quiet and he studied the terrain around the herd to see how best to approach them for a shot. The buffalo were in a small basin with a series of drainage gullies that fed in and out. Francis saw that the one that ran off to the east seemed to provide the best course. It was deep and wound back toward him in a big loop, with a smaller ditch he could use for access. He nodded and pointed with his chin.

"See that ditch off to the right?" He looked at Lottie, then back. "You go back with Billy, I'll make my way down there and— "

Suddenly, as if by magic, there was a burst of gray smoke below them from the edge of the gully that pointed toward the buffalo. Half an instant later Francis heard the crack of a rifle—they were so far away it took that long for the sound to reach them—and one of the cows watching the fighting bulls pitched forward and down onto her side.

"What . . ."

There was another puff of smoke. Another cow went down; then another shot, and another and another, coming so fast they were almost on top of each other, and each time, a cow would drop on her side and start kicking in death. Twelve shots. Twelve cows.

"Francis, somebody is shooting our buffalo!" Lottie punched his shoulder.

"Stay down." Francis watched the basin below. The buffalo had not run but were moving in confused circles. "And quiet—be quiet and let's see what's going on." Twelve shots in perhaps twenty seconds. No man on earth could load and fire a muzzle-loading rifle thirty-six times a minute. There had to be more than one man hiding in the gully. Francis looked to the rear and waved to Billy—who had heard the shooting—to stay where he was with the horses.

"There!" Lottie whispered. "There they are."

Francis couldn't believe his eyes. A tall, thin man in a full dark suit came out of the gully, followed by three other men in tan suits, all wearing strange-looking round helmets. The man in the dark suit carried nothing, but the other three had two rifles each and were festooned with powder horns and belts and ramrods.

"Why, Francis, he's a fancy man." Lottie snorted. "What's a fancy man doing way out here?"

"Killing buffalo, the way it looks." Francis studied them a moment, wondered if there was danger there, decided there could not be and shrugged. "They seem harmless. Let's go down and see why they needed to shoot a dozen buffalo."

——— Chapter Two ———

Francis and Lottie walked back to Billy and mounted up. As they rode down, Francis explained what they had seen to Billy.

The rest of the herd had fled with the approach of the four men, and Francis stopped in front of the man in the dark suit, who was leaning—Francis had to work to keep himself from staring—on a silver-headed cane. Behind the man with the cane, Francis could see yet another man in a tan uniform back in the gully, who had been hidden before. He was holding five horses and two pack mules.

"Oh, I say." The man in the suit spoke in a strange accent. "This is smashing, absolutely *smashing*. What luck. We'll have guests for dinner! Do say you'll join us, won't you? We're going to have a mountain of fresh tongue. . . ."

"My name is Francis, this is Lottie and the boy back there is named Billy."

"Oh, do forgive me. My name is Bentley. William James Bentley the Fourth, actually. And these men are my servants."

Francis nodded, speechless. Billy heeled his horse forward until it was next to Francis. He had become incredibly accurate with his bow—had indeed once helped to save Francis and Lottie from Courtweiler and Dubs. Now Billy sat with the bow across his lap, an arrow nocked to the string.

"He talks funny," Billy said to Francis. "Sort of like them others we had to shoot . . ."

Francis nodded at Bentley. "You do have a kind of . . . accent—"

"I'm English," Bentley said, interrupting. "We're from England on a grand adventure before I take over the estate from my parents."

"A grand adventure . . ." For a second images jolted through Francis's mind. Jason Grimes scalping Braid, Comancheros, the Mexican War; himself being held captive by Pawnee, freezing, being shot at, snakebit. Shooting and burying people.

"Why, yes. Your Oregon Trail is quite the thing in England. Stories of the trail and the wilderness abound. We came over last year and wintered in Independence, where we also outfitted, although I brought my own rifles. They were made by a superb gunsmith named Drills. Then we started west with pack mules. . . ."

This man, thought Francis, actually talks more than Lottie.

"And made rather good time, what with this absolutely capital early spring and all the grass for the livestock, much better time than we would have made pulling wagons . . ."

Francis held up his hand. "Please, just a minute."

"Let him talk, Francis," Lottie said. "His voice is pretty, like a bird."

Francis shook his head. "Do you have a guide?"

"Why?" Bentley shrugged. "One simply travels west."

Francis sighed. He was hoping for a guide to tell him how far north they had to go to hit the trail. "You mean you've come all this way with no guide?"

"Assuredly. Although we may have missed some of the more noteworthy aspects of the journey without proper guidance. We have not, for instance, seen any red Indians. One would like to see some red Indians. Are they, for instance, really red?"

Francis thought back again to Braid, to the Comancheros. Oh my yes, let us see some red Indians.

He pulled his thinking back to the present. "You shot twelve buffalo."

"Quite. My men reloaded for me so that I could just keep firing. Splendid, what? Mind you, it's not as good as back in the grass prairie. We had a day when we shot seventy-two of the great beasts. It was capital, simply capital."

"Why?" Francis couldn't help himself. "What did you do with them?"

"Took the tongues, of course. We dried some

and pickled some and ate some fresh. It's the very best meat, tongue."

Billy couldn't stand it. "All the rest was left to rot?"

Bentley shrugged. "There are millions of them."

We have to get away from this man, Francis thought. He's friendly enough but he stinks of death. Just that—death.

"You will join us for dinner, won't you?" Bentley asked again.

Francis shook his head. "I'm sorry but we have to keep riding." Out of the corner of his eye he saw Lottie throw him a sharp look but for once she remained quiet. "We have to get north and west to Oregon before fall. But if you don't mind, I would like to get some hump meat and grease off one of those buffalo you killed."

"Of course, of course. My men will help you, and you can even take some tongue if you wish."

"No, just back meat and grease. You don't have to help, it will just take a minute."

Francis moved to a young cow. He would not have shot her himself—she was just over a year old and too young to kill—but since she was dead anyway and he knew the meat would be tender, he decided to use her. He cut down the center of the back and took out the hump and the tenderloins that ran down both sides of the backbone. He also removed the skin from both sides—Lottie helped him while Billy held the horses—and then rolled the cow over and cut her belly open and took several long strips of belly fat. The whole operation didn't take fifteen minutes. The meat was rolled in the green hide and packed on the packhorse.

Francis remounted his own horse and stopped in front of Bentley. He felt he should say something to the Englishman. It was a pure miracle the man and his servants had managed to come this far without running into hostile Indians or, worse, scavengers who worked the trail, preying on travelers the way Courtweiler and Dubs had done.

"Mr. Bentley, don't go much more south. If you go too far that way, you will run into the Comancheros."

"Oh, are they red Indians?"

Francis nodded. "There are some Indians with them but mostly they are plain mean and will kill you for your shoes, let alone those pretty rifles. You should head back north and hook up with a wagon train. There's safety in numbers."

Bentley smiled and held out his hand to shake. "Well, I thank you for the advice, my boy, but there are five of us and as you can see we are heavily armed. I don't think we need to fear."

Francis shook his head. "Mr. Bentley . . ." Then he realized it would do no good to say more, so he shook hands with Bentley and nudged his horse and rode away.

Within a hundred yards Billy had moved well off to the side and ahead, scouting, and Lottie had pulled her horse and the packhorse, which she trailed, up alongside Francis.

"I think we could have stayed for food, though to be honest I don't think I would much favor tongue, but he talked so pretty, Francis, I could have listened to him for hours and hours and maybe he would have cooked something other than tongue if we'd asked him nice enough and maybe he even had potatoes. Oh, Francis, wouldn't a potato taste wonderful? I swear, I haven't had a potato in so long I've forgotten what they taste like. . . ."

And she went on and on, but Francis could

not shake the smell of death that had been on Bentley, and he heeled his pony to a faster walk.

The farther they could get from Bentley the better.

—— Chapter Three ——

"I saw dust." Billy came in from the right side, where he had been riding in a parallel line about a mile away. He urged his pony into a lope until he was next to Francis and Lottie. It was late afternoon and his horse was sweating from the heat.

"How far off?" They had come two days since meeting Bentley, and Francis still felt too close to the hunter. He could not help thinking that Bentley would draw something bad to himself, and Francis did not want to be around when it happened.

"I'm not sure. I don't know distances."

"If you're walking a horse, how long would you have to walk to get to the dust?"

Billy frowned, thinking. "Maybe an hour . . ."

Three miles, perhaps four. "Where are they?"

"Off to the side, moving the same way we are, heading north."

"How big is the dust cloud?"

Another frown. "Hard to tell. Maybe the same as three or four buffalo might make walking—more than we make but not a whole lot either."

"What do you think?" This came from Lottie.

But Francis was still intent upon Billy: "How fast are they moving?"

"They came up even with us at a pretty good clip, then they seemed to let up and are holding, the same as us."

"Are they Comancheros?" Lottie looked grim. "Could it be them?"

Francis shook his head. "I don't think so. They usually move in big groups. This seems like a smaller bunch: four, five men at the most." He looked back at their own trail. If Billy can see their dust maybe they can see ours, he thought. But they had been moving largely through grassy meadows where there was no dust, and the other group—whoever they were—were farther east, in the foothills of the mountains where there was less grass and more dry dirt.

"What do we do?" Lottie peered eastward, trying to see the dust.

"Nothing right now. It might even be Bentley and his men taking my advice and going north. We'll wait until dark and I'll sneak over and see who they are."

"I'll go too," Billy said.

"Not this time. I need you here to keep an eye on things with Lottie."

"But I'm good at sneaking. . . ."

"I know. But one is enough for this kind of work. I'm going on foot and you can help keep the horses here."

Billy frowned but at last nodded. "All right, but I don't like it."

"It's for the best, Billy," Lottie added.

And in a terrible way, that proved to be right.

★ ★ ★

THERE WAS A SLIVER of moon, no clouds and a sky packed with stars—enough light so that Francis could see just shadows and shapes.

"No fire tonight," he told Lottie. "Eat some of the venison jerky cold."

She nodded. Billy was near the horses, sulking.

"You watch out for snakes," she said. Francis had been bitten by a rattler while trying to sneak up on a Pueblo village and it had nearly killed him.

Francis nodded, checked his rifle to make certain the cap was firmly seated on the nipple and set off in an easy shuffle. He would have preferred taking a horse, but it would whinny when it smelled the other horses and give him away.

The country was rolling hills, but they were small and well rounded, so the going was easy. He could have made good time but he opted for caution. Instead of making for the strange camp in a straight line he looped slightly north and moved slowly, stopping often to listen and watch the shadows.

When he had walked about three miles, he caught a flicker of light. He stopped and watched it until he knew it was a campfire. It was more than a mile away and he could tell that whoever it was who'd made it had no concept of caution. The fire was huge, and showers of sparks leaped into the air as whole logs were tossed onto the blaze.

Bentley, Francis thought. It must be him. Still, he had to be sure, and keeping a low profile, he worked his way closer until he was no more than thirty yards from them. He crouched in a small ditch and watched.

It was indeed Bentley and his men. Francis shook his head. They must have taken his advice to head north, but their camping methods were nothing short of insane.

Even in good times it paid to be cautious. Always—unless you were in a cave or a well-concealed ditch—you *always* kept your fire small and burning clean. No spark, no light, must get out to show itself to possible enemies. And that was in good times. Right now, in the aftermath of the Mexican War, when the Comancheros were raiding and other scavengers were about, being careful was the only way to stay alive.

Francis lay watching them for nearly half an hour as they laughed and joked, throwing still more wood on the fire. At last he decided he should let them know he was there and tell them how foolish they were being. Then he froze.

At first he couldn't tell what caused him to stop. Some instinct made him hold up, freeze, and then let his eyes move away from the fire.

There.

A soft line that shouldn't be there, a curve of a shadow against the dark. Then a sound, a soft clink of metal against stone. For the time it took to draw three more breaths, there was nothing strange at all.

When it came, it was so fast and so brutal Francis almost cried out. If he had, it would have been his last act on earth.

Out of the shadows, out of the dark night, a pack of devils appeared. Later Francis decided it must have been five men, but it happened so fast he couldn't count them.

At first there was no time to move, to warn Bentley's group, and then, within seconds, Francis didn't dare.

The men were armed with guns at their belts, wearing ragged clothes and old floppy army hats. But they did not use their guns. Three men also carried army sabers, and the two others had lances.

There were almost no sounds. The attackers were on the group in an instant, hacking and stabbing with silent ferocity.

It was a massacre and it was over in moments. Bentley and his men were dead almost at once. Still the attackers did not stop, but kept hacking and chopping and tearing until the bodies were in pieces, the heads chopped off and all the clothing removed. Francis lay in his small ditch in the dark, horrified, not believing what he was seeing, though he knew it was real.

All this time, the men were silent. Then one, apparently the leader, stood spattered in blood in the light of the fire and said, "I wonder who they were?"

Another man answered. "I don't know, but they sure had good rifles. Look at these guns!"

Francis was still afraid to move. He stayed where he was until the men found some whiskey and started drinking. He waited until they were drunk. Only then, a few hours later, did he crawl backward on his belly until he could crouch, then moved along in that crouch until he could stand. And then he turned and started off in a silent trot, which soon became an outright run.

And not for a second could he get the last sight out of his mind: Bentley's head jammed on the end of a lance, the light from the fire giving it a hideous glow that made it look almost still alive.

Chapter Four

"We have to stop, Francis." Lottie's voice was strident. "You're going to kill the horses!"

Francis seemed not to hear her or to care about what she said—even if there was an edge of truth in it.

He had come back to them just at dawn and found them both dozing, with Billy holding the horses' picket rope.

"Up!" Francis had rousted them out of sleep. "We have to start moving. *Now!*"

"But, Francis . . ." Lottie had rubbed her eyes. "What is it? Why . . ."

Francis had looked at her but all he could see was Bentley's head, all he could think of was the mad dance of the murderers hacking and slashing and stabbing. I am here, he'd thought. With all that I have in the world to live for—Lottie and Billy. The hope of finding my family. All the Spanish gold and silver from the old grave. We are here, and madmen are . . . right . . . over . . . *there.*

Insane butchers are just four or five miles away. They're worse than Comancheros, worse than attacking bears or Indians—they are like wolves with rabies. They kill just to kill.

Francis had hurried to get Billy and Lottie away from them.

"Bad men," he had told Lottie and Billy. He did not tell them what he had seen. He would never tell them what he had seen. Not if he lived to be a hundred years old.

"We have to run. Now!"

He had kept them to grass so there would be no dust as they rode, and he'd driven them hard all day. He thought the killers would head north and maybe a little east to catch the wagon trains, looking for small parties to attack, and so he'd taken Lottie and Billy northwest. At first he'd led them but as the mounts tired, he dropped back and pushed them, whipped them until it was dark. And still he drove them. All night, with the horses staggering, until dawn came again, and he thought they had traveled close to fifty miles. And at last he stopped near a beaver pond in a stand of aspen with the morning sun warming the horses' sweat so that it steamed.

"We stop here," he said. "Cold camp, no fire—eat jerky and sleep. Five, six hours. Billy, you sleep tied to the horses like you did before."

He left them and with his rifle went to the top of a nearby hill and squatted, looking out across the foothills.

He was exhausted, almost staggering, like the horses. But he sat for an hour, not moving, hardly blinking, hearing the flies around him, the birds, the squirrels, beaver—staring at their back trail and the hills to the east.

Nothing. No dust, no movement. Nothing. And finally, while he stared, his eyes closed once, opened slowly, then closed again. He fell backward and slept.

HE WAS NOT CERTAIN what awakened him. It was close to evening; he had slept hard for nearly seven hours and probably could have slept for seven more. Lottie and Billy were still asleep, the horses standing asleep near them. As he watched, a horse awoke and started to move, eating great mouthfuls of grass that he tore off with sideways motions. The horse came to the end of the picket line and jerked Billy—who had the rope tied to his wrist—along in the dirt for a good two feet.

Billy did not wake up, and Francis smiled. All right, the trail seemed clear. The horses needed to eat and rest more and recover. They would spend the night and move on in the morning.

He studied the horizon one more time and found it clear, stood and stretched and made his way down to the horses. They were all awake and whickered softly as he untied the picket line from Billy's wrist—Billy still did not wake—and led them softly into tall grass. There he hobbled them with rope and let them graze.

The beaver pond was nearby, and for no particular reason he walked to it and stood looking into the clear water. He could see trout, their sides flashing in the sun, and as he turned to go he caught another glint.

This was at the edge of the pond near the horses, where the beaver dragged the cut limbs into the water and left a muddy skid trail on the bank.

A gray flicker of light from the sun cut into the water and he knew instantly that it was a trap. He moved to it through the grass without stepping in any dirt, reading signs now, studying. He had trapped beaver with a man named Jason Grimes. Grimes had helped Francis escape from the Pawnees who had taken him from the wagon train so long ago. Mr. Grimes had shown up again at the Comancheros camp and helped the three of them escape and then had led the Comancheros off while Lottie and Billy and Francis ran north.

Francis stopped by the bank and studied the trap in open disbelief.

Because he only had one arm, Jason Grimes had a unique way of tying the small aspen bait stick to the pan of the trap. He used a bit of rawhide in a crisscross fashion because he had to hold the trap with his knee while he tied the rawhide with one hand.

Francis was looking down at just such a knot now. He leaned closer. The bait stick was fresh-cut —not more than two days old—and the trap was not covered with leaves and debris as it would have been if it had been there a long time. Besides, Grimes would never put traps where he couldn't check them every day. It wouldn't be fair to the animal to let it suffer in the trap.

Francis stood, looked to his left carefully and started swinging his eyes to the right, looking into the trees, trying to see past the green leaves of the aspens, then moving to the left again, searching in increments, carefully studying each part before moving to the next, and before he had gone halfway around he heard a soft voice say:

"Well, pilgrim, I see you got clear of them Comancheros."

And Francis wheeled to see Jason Grimes standing in the dappled shade of the aspens.

———— Chapter Five ————

"How—I mean when . . ." Francis shrugged and sighed. "Hello, Mr. Grimes, it is good to see you." He was surprised and shouldn't have been. Nothing the mountain man ever did should surprise him. "How did you come to be here?"

Grimes stepped forward and matched Francis's smile. "Same as you, boy. Same as you."

In the light, out of the shade, Francis saw Grimes clearly, and was shocked to see that he looked thin and wasted, as if half starved. There was a new scar from his left cheekbone up to his hairline. His hair was also spotty and turning white. Francis looked away at once but not before Grimes caught his expression.

"I made it clear of the Comancheros," he said, "when they were chasing us. Or almost clear. Two of them were right pushy and kept coming; I cornered up and dealt with them but one of them caught me with a hand ax while I worked on him. . . . Dust."

For a second Francis didn't follow him. He saw that the ax wound had healed, but that didn't explain the way Grimes looked—near death.

"There," Grimes repeated. "Dust. Coming this way."

Francis turned and looked where Grimes was pointing—three or four miles to the east, out of the foothills on the edge of the prairie—and saw a small plume of dust and he thought, *Oh God*, and it wasn't swearing but a prayer.

"Not like you to pray," Grimes said, and Francis realized he'd said it aloud. "Not over a little dust . . ."

"It's not just the dust." Francis squinted, trying to see better. "It's what's making the dust. Or at least what I think is making it."

"Five men," Grimes said. "Crazy—like wolves with crazy-water sickness. Is that right?"

"You know about them?"

Grimes nodded. "Heard about them. They came from back east—Tennessee or some such hill place. They've been running and killing out here for nearly two years. They were in the army and came out for the war but broke loose and went bad. Real bad."

"I have to wake the others, get the horses ready to run again. You can come with us."

But Grimes wasn't listening. He stared fixedly at the dust plume and seemed to be thinking. Then he squatted on his haunches and smoothed the dirt at his feet and took a stick for a pointer.

"See this canyon here—the one we're in?" He drew a shallow V with the stick in the dirt. "It goes back into the peaks and looks like a dead end, but it ain't. I found this canyon when I came north, after I got away from those Comancheros, and I wintered here, trapped a little beaver just for the meat." He inhaled and for the first time Francis noted how he was wheezing and having trouble catching his breath. "You take the young ones back up the canyon and you'll find a trail out the back. It looks snowed in but it ain't."

Francis nodded. "Good. Let's get going."

But Grimes smiled and shook his head. "I ain't going."

"What do you mean?" Francis pointed toward the dust. "They'll be here in an hour. You can't get away from them by heading out the front of the canyon."

"I'm not going to try to get away from them. Fact is, ever since I heard of them I've kind of been hoping I'd run into them."

"But . . . but *why?* They'll kill you. Believe me, I saw what they do. They'll cut you to pieces."

Grimes nodded. "There's that possibility, Mr. Tucket."

"Then why stay? Come with us, run with us."

Grimes looked at the dust—it was closer now by a mile—and then looked back up the canyon at the snow-covered peaks, seemed to see something up there, up in the mountains. "No. This is as good a place as any to die—better than most."

"Die?" Francis stared at him. "Why stay here and die?"

"Because I'm dying anyway—been wasting away for months. I'm about done now—it's all I can do to walk. I cut my horses loose to run three weeks ago."

"What?" Francis paused, his breathing suddenly shallow. "Not you, Mr. Grimes!"

"I got somethin' tearing at my vitals. At least now I won't have to just rot away. I can get those five scavengers to help me while I take a few of them with me."

"No!" Francis shook his head. "There are doctors. We have money—gold. Lots of gold. We can get help."

Grimes smiled. "Not this time, Mr. Tucket. Not this time. You go wake the children and be on your way now, before they pick up your trail and start to gain on you."

"But—"

"No buts to it. Get to riding if you want to save the young ones. You ain't got twenty minutes left. Besides, I've got work to do. I've got to pick a place to make my last . . . to make my stand."

"I'll stay. Two guns are better than one."

Again Grimes shook his head, this time slowly. "That won't work and you know it. If they get past us they'll get the children. They stay to fight me, that will give you time to run, and even if I don't stop them I'll guarantee you that all five won't be coming on."

Francis stood there for a count of ten, tried to make it work in his mind, tried to think of a way to stay and help, but he knew Grimes was right. Hated that Grimes was right but knew it. He still could not bring himself to leave his friend. "I'll send the others on. They'll get away."

"Get away. Now. Go." Grimes looked at the dust again. "They've stopped." And now a new sound came into his voice. It was as if Francis weren't there and Grimes were standing alone. His body seemed to uncoil in some way, and he stood taller and his eyes grew hard and he squinted tightly. "There, they're coming on. Maybe saw one of your tracks. Five of them. Ready to kill." He smiled. "That ought to be about right. I always said it would take at least five men to finish me. . . . We'll see, we'll see. . . ." He turned and saw Francis and seemed surprised. "You still here? Get gone. Now. It's going to get interesting around here in about half an hour."

Francis hung there for another five seconds,

tearing at it in his mind, and then he knew Grimes was right, and he turned and ran to wake Lottie and Billy.

They were used to reacting quickly now, and within four minutes were mounted and the three of them were riding, with Lottie wisely remaining silent and Billy offering to go back and fight, alone if necessary, and insistent enough that Francis thought he would have to tie the boy across his horse before he could make him come. Billy gave in at last only because Lottie joined forces with Francis and convinced him it would be best to come.

They went past where Grimes had been but Francis could not see him and knew he was getting ready. Francis peered into the trees but couldn't see any sign. That did not mean Grimes wasn't there. The old mountain man would be finding his best fighting ground—his back covered in some way, his rifle loaded and checked, a second and third load of lead balls and patches in his mouth to reload quickly, his knife and ax to hand. Getting ready. Ready.

He looked up into the mountains where the trail Grimes had pointed to worked out of the back of the canyon. He tried to focus on it, see it amid the peaks, visualize how it must lie, and tried not to look back. He rode that way with Lottie and Billy for a time, letting his horse pick out a faint path. At last he could stand it no longer and he looked back.

They had climbed, and the valley lay before him. The dust had disappeared, which meant that the men had either stopped or come into the grass where there would be no dust. He thought they had kept coming, and he tried to gauge how far they had moved and tried again not to think of what was going to happen, to think only of keeping Lottie's and Billy's horses moving ahead of him. He was forcing his mind to look ahead when the first shot came from below and he could not stand it, would not stand it.

"Keep moving up the trail!" he yelled at Lottie and Billy, and wheeled his horse and slammed the barrel of his rifle across her rump and was gone back down the trail.

To the mountain man, to Jason Grimes.

Chapter Six

The mare ran hard because it was downhill and because she was fresh and because Francis kept hitting her across the rear with the barrel of his rifle. He knew it did not help—she was running as fast as she could, mouth wide, spit flying back—but he could not help himself.

After the first shot there was a small delay— perhaps thirty seconds—and then a second shot. In those thirty seconds Francis's pony covered a quarter of a mile. After the second shot, another short delay, and then a third shot followed by two more in rapid succession.

Francis ran toward the gunfire and came around a small stand of aspen into a long, narrow clearing.

The grass and trees were green. He would always remember the green. The sun came through the trees and the light gathered the color and seemed to bathe the whole clearing in a green glow. Everything else seemed frozen, as in a tableau.

Far down the clearing, near the other end, a horse wandered aimlessly, chewing at grass, still saddled and bridled. The body of a man lay on the ground near the horse.

Halfway down the clearing another horse stood, still saddled and bridled, and beside him another man lay unmoving in the grass.

Closer in, a third horse stood and on the ground near him a man sat, with a red stain on his chest just above the stomach, and he was looking down at it. As Francis watched, he fell over sideways, still looking at the stain.

Closer still, near where Francis and the mare came storming out of the trees, a fourth man lay with Grimes's hand ax embedded in his head.

Nearer yet, almost beneath the pinto's hooves, Grimes knelt with the fifth man, the two of them facing each other, Grimes with his head down slightly, as if working, and his hunting knife deep in the center of the man, holding him up in a kneeling position—though the man was clearly dead.

All five, Francis thought. He killed all five in not one full minute. Two shot long, one closer in, one with his tomahawk and the knife at the end.

"You're . . . you're something," Francis said, sliding off his horse. "You're just something. All five of them—"

Grimes raised his head and Francis saw it: Grimes had been hit. Hit once across his left shoulder, and again through the left side of his chest. When he raised his head Francis could also see the other man's knife in Grimes's side, up under the left ribs into the lung.

"I'm shot and cut to pieces, Mr. Tucket. It appears I got my wish." He pushed the other man away and tried to stand but instead he fell onto his side.

Francis was next to him. "Where . . . what can I do?"

Grimes seemed not to hear. He struggled to rise and at last, with Francis helping, he made it to a sitting position. Francis could see blood coming out of the corner of his mouth now and he knew the mountain man's lungs were gone, knew it was over.

"You lie back." Francis moved to help him. "We'll make camp here and feed you and make some bandages. You'll be good in a week, maybe two. I'll get some hump meat for you. . . ."

Grimes shook his head. "Let me be. Just let me be." He was quiet again, pulling air hard, leaning against Francis, who was crying openly. Grimes's breathing stopped and Francis thought he was gone, but it started again and Grimes said, "Don't you bury me. Leave me for the wolves and coyotes."

"But it isn't—"

"Don't. I want them to have me and take me on with them. Leave me out of the ground."

He was silent for another long time, his breath coming ragged, and then he looked at Francis, into his eyes, and he said, "I wish I could see one more sunrise," and he died then, with Francis holding him in the green light and with the bodies he had conquered all around him, died without closing his eyes, and Francis stared down at him and thought he could not stand it. Something, some part of what made him alive, had been cut out of him with Grimes's death and he could not hear and he could not see and he thought of his love for Grimes and his hatred for the men who had killed him, and of the green light and of Grimes fighting Braid and trapping beaver and saving Francis from the Pawnees and again from the Comancheros and from these five men, and he cried and cried, heaving with it, until Lottie and Billy came back to find him and put a blanket over him while he sat for the day and all the night, holding the dead mountain man, crying for what he had lost.

—— Chapter Seven ——

Francis sat his horse on a ridge between two clear-white peaks that shot up into a blue sky and thought of an Indian prayer he had heard.

> *There is beauty above me,*
> *There is beauty below me,*
> *All around me there is beauty.*

The peaks went out ahead of him as if they were marching to the west. Huge, craggy mountains were still fully coated in snow. And he knew that probably no man from the east had seen them except for Grimes and perhaps other wandering mountain men. Grimes had told him once that Kit Carson had said he'd been out here, but that might have been something Kit made up. The word was he made many things up.

"Why are we stopping?" Lottie came up beside Francis. "There's no wood here for a fire and no water for the horses either. Shouldn't we go on down into the valley a little?"

Francis shrugged. It had been four days since Grimes had died and Francis was still, as Billy said quietly to Lottie the first night, ". . . not right in the head."

It was not just the death of Grimes, although that had triggered it. They had done as Grimes had asked and sat him at the base of a tree with his rifle across his lap and his ax and knife close to hand by his side, leaning back against the tree so he could see out across the prairie to the horizon.

The other five bodies Francis had roped and dragged, one at a time, to a gully. He dumped them in and left them.

He'd searched them first. Even in grief he could not bring himself to waste anything. They had the rifles they had stolen from the English-man and some gold coins and the odd striker and flint to make sparks and start a fire but little else. He did not know what to do with the rifles. He was used to his own and did not like the foreign look of them. They were huge long-barreled af-fairs impossible to handle well on a horse and he offered one to Billy, who picked it up and found that it was much longer than he was tall and put it down.

"I'll stay with my bow," he said. He had hunted with the bow ever since they'd stayed at the Pueblo village and his arrows kept them in camp meat—turkey, rabbits, squirrels and even one deer.

In the end, they left the rifles near Grimes. The packhorse was already encumbered with food and gold and the rifles were just extra weight they could not carry.

And so they had ridden away from Grimes, but Francis could not shake the feeling of an end to some part of his life he could not understand, as if he had somehow died with the mountain man. They had followed the trail Grimes had told them of but had made slow time because Francis stopped frequently to stare at the peaks and remember his life with Grimes, sometimes dismounting and sitting for half a day, holding the reins to his horse, gazing at nothing.

He left everything to Billy and Lottie. Setting up camp, killing and cooking meat, finding the trail—which was not well marked—and even scouting for possible danger. He would stop in the evenings when and where Lottie said to stop, sit while they gathered wood and struck a flint to make fire, eat what Lottie handed him to eat, drink when he was thirsty, or not, if water wasn't at hand.

On this fourth night he did not sleep, as he had not slept the previous three nights, and on this fourth night Grimes came to him.

Francis was sitting, looking into the fire. It had died down to a bed of red coals. Lottie and Billy were wrapped in their blankets, sleeping deeply, turned away from the flames, and Francis wasn't thinking of anything in particular except to wonder if he would ever sleep again, and Grimes came walking in and sat down by the fire pit.

Francis jumped back, thinking: A ghost! But Grimes did not show any wounds. He sat quietly for some time looking at the glowing coals, as Francis had been doing, and then he looked up and said softly, as if worrying that he might wake the other two:

"It's all right."

"What?" Francis leaned toward him. "What did you say?"

But Grimes stood, hefted his rifle so that it lay cradled in his one good arm, nodded at Francis and walked into the darkness without looking back.

Francis watched him until he was out of sight. Then he sighed and smiled and lay down on his side and was instantly, profoundly and deeply asleep.

HE AWAKENED to find himself covered with a blanket, his rifle at his side. It was still dark and Lottie had a fire going and was cooking a whole rear leg of venison on a spit over the flames.

Francis raised himself on one elbow. "That's quite a bit of meat for breakfast."

His voice startled her and she jumped and scowled at him. "You nearly scared me to death. And for your information it's not breakfast. This is supper. You slept the clock around—all night and all day until dark again."

Francis lay back and, looked at the fire silently for a time. He did not feel lost as he had before, did not feel ended. He could hear and smell the meat cooking and could hear the night sounds around them. Nearby the horses were standing, picketed, and he could hear them breathing. Off to the west a coyote yipped. "Grimes came to me," he said.

"Came to you?" Lottie stopped turning the meat. "You mean in a dream?"

"He means a ha'nt." Billy was sitting across the fire wiping grease into his bowstring. It was made from twisted deer-leg tendon and it dried out if not kept greased. "Grimes came as a ha'nt . . . a ghost."

"No." Francis sat up. "He came and sat next to me and told me it was all right. Then he got up and left and then I went to sleep."

"It was a ha'nt," Billy repeated. "He was worried about you and was coming back to tell you it was all right. Ha'nts ain't all bad. Some of them are good."

"What do you know about ghosts?" Lottie said. "It's all stuff and nonsense. If Francis said Grimes came back to him, then Mr. Grimes came back to him, and if he said it's going to be all right, it's going to be all right. You go check the horses, make sure they're still picketed right, while Francis and me think on what to do next."

Billy hesitated, but something in her eye made him think better of speaking and he went to do as she said. She turned to Francis as soon as the boy was gone.

"Are you really all right, Francis? Because you haven't been yourself for days and days."

He held up his hand. "I'm fine."

She turned the deer leg slowly. The fat dripping from it into the open flame sputtered and flashed as it ignited. "I was worried about you."

He lay back and closed his eyes. "I'm all right. Don't worry. I'm fine now. We'll eat and sleep another night and then tomorrow we'll strike north as best we can and see if we can find the wagon trail that Grimes said was there." His stomach rumbled. "But for now, how much more are we going to cook that meat? I could eat dirt."

Lottie smiled. He was back.

Chapter Eight

Francis held his horse back below the crest of a small rise, dismounted and went to her nose and pinched it so she wouldn't whinny. Two miles back Lottie and Billy were following. Ahead of him, over the rise and a mile away, there appeared to be a man on horseback with a herd of twenty or twenty-five horses that he was pushing ahead of him. The man had a saddle and was not an Indian, but Francis was wary, especially of someone alone out here with horses in a herd.

He walked and led his horse until his eyes came just over the ridge, where he could see without being seen. He watched for a good fifteen minutes. The man wasn't pushing his little herd but seemed to be letting them graze along at their own speed.

Francis heard a sound and turned to see Lottie and Billy approach. He motioned them to stop well back but it was too late. Billy's pony smelled the herd and cut loose with a shrill whinny— almost a scream.

The effect on the man a mile away was immediate and strange.

He galloped his mount around the herd, got them moving straight away from Francis and then he took out a bugle and blew a series of high notes, one rapidly after another, and in what seemed seconds a group of five men on horses came boiling over yet another ridge to surround the horse herd in a protective circle.

It was all done very efficiently and looked so controlled and disciplined that something about it reassured Francis—he even thought they might be Army—and he remounted and showed himself above the ridge. When Lottie and Billy caught up they rode toward the herd.

As they grew closer Francis waved, and one man waved back and came riding out to meet them.

He was not Army but he rode a good mount, well taken care of, had a good rifle, also well cared for—a large, beefy man with rounded shoulders and huge hands—and he smiled when he saw them. "Why, you are but sprites. Are you alone in the wilderness at such an early age?"

Francis said, "We came from south a ways. Did you come from back east this year?"

The man nodded. "I am Orson, and these men are Caleb, Lyle, John, James and Isaiah. We are heading west for the promised land in the golden valley by the Columbia River. Are you children of God?"

Francis wasn't sure how to answer but Lottie came forward and said, "We are all children of God, that's what my mother said before we were attacked and all killed but my brother and me, saved by Francis here."

Francis looked at her sharply. Her mother had died of croup. Her father had taken the children westward two years later and died of cholera; she and Billy had been cast out by the wagon train.

He thought she shouldn't lie but she gave him a look right back as if to say, "Do you *want* me to tell them our father had cholera?" and went on. "Which was over a year ago and since then we've been captured by the army, then the evil Comancheros, escaped at great peril, been attacked by wild men and bitten by snakes. . . ."

The man named Orson held up his hand. "That's enough. You must come and visit with us for a time and tell us the stories."

There was something about the man, something so open and honest that Francis said, "It would be nice if we could team up with you. To get west. I have folks out there somewhere I need to find. I'm a fair hunter and Billy is as good a scout as you'll ever meet and Lottie can help the womenfolk." He got a definite scowl here. "Why, she can run your whole camp."

Orson nodded. "We'd be glad of the company but we have no womenfolk. We left them all back home while we came out ahead to settle the land. They'll come in a year or so by ship, down around Cape Horn and back up, to meet us where the river runs into the Pacific Ocean. And if you can hunt you'll be more than welcome. We can shoot game when it's plentiful but it seems to have pulled back from the trail and we can't get close enough for a shot."

They had been riding while they spoke, and they came up over a small rise now. Francis could see a small group of wagons—he counted six of them—arranged in a circle with oxen herded into the middle. So they were using oxen to pull the wagons and had just brought the horses for . . . what?

"Why so many horses if you aren't pulling the wagons with them?"

Orson smiled. "We were told there's a shortage of good horses out west and we pooled what money we had and brought these mares and some stallions for brood stock. We hope to sell horses as well as to farm."

Francis nodded but thought it perhaps a little bit silly. The West was covered with horses, small mustangs, wild Indian ponies, that were as tough and good as any he'd ever seen, but even as he had the thought he found himself looking at some of Orson's stock with envy. They were large, well muscled and strong-looking, not just for riding but for all-around work, pulling a wagon or cultivator or even a single-bottom plow.

Look at me, he thought, thinking like a farmer. Grimes would roll over in his grave. If he had a grave—the thought jumped into his mind. The way Grimes had looked sitting against the trees, his eyes glazed and staring out across the prairie . . . He shook his head. That was how the mountain man had wanted it and it was right for him, right for the wolves to carry him off.

"We have some hump meat," Francis said. They had taken a buffalo the day before, a young cow with new spring fat on her, and had twenty pounds of fresh meat wrapped in green hide. "We'll cook that for food tonight and Billy and I will start scouting and hunting in the morning."

Orson nodded. "Roast buffalo hump sounds as good as Christmas dinner. We still have potatoes to boil. . . ."

"You have potatoes?" This from Lottie. "Oh my, I haven't had boiled potatoes with gravy for, oh my, I can't remember when. . . ."

And so that night for the first time in what seemed years, Francis prayed before eating (or at least listened to the others pray) and ate meat cut in slices from a pan with a fork, and ate boiled potatoes covered in buffalo-fat brown gravy that Lottie made in a cast-iron pot by burning some flour in grease and adding water to thicken it, ate until he could eat no more and listened to the men talking of the farms they would make when they came to the golden valley, their voices mixing with each other in a kind of low music, until he curled up in the dirt by the fire to sleep.

He supposed that Grimes would have called these men pilgrims, with a cutting edge to his voice. But Francis's last thought was that all of it, the talk and the dreams of farms and the civilized food, all of it set well with him and he didn't mind.

─── Chapter Nine ───

He had never seen people work so hard. In truth, everybody who came west on the trains had to work a great deal just to cover the ground, but these men, all big, all happy, ready to laugh or pray, whichever mood took them, worked until he thought they would drop. If something broke they fixed it, and fixed it better than it had been when it was new. Or if something looked like it was going to break, they would fix it. If a horse came to the edge of limping, even hesitated in its step, they were on it and working at the hooves, checking it, rubbing liniment into its skin, slowing its pace, talking to it in low, reassuring sounds that seemed almost like music.

"They . . . they love things," Lottie said to Francis one day when they'd been traveling with the men about a week.

"What do you mean?" Francis was cleaning his rifle and looked up.

"The men. Watch them. They love everything. They love horses and oxen and wagons and when they talk about their families at night they love them and the mountains even when it's hard going . . . they just seem to love things."

And when he thought of it Francis agreed. He never heard a bad word from the men. One morning they were greasing wagon axles, taking each wooden wheel off with the axle propped up on a fork and wiping the wooden axle with buffalo grease, and one of the wagons fell on Orson's foot. It caught the edge of his foot and caused a nasty cut and a huge bruise. Francis thought it must have hurt like blue blazes but Orson merely stood there until they pulled the wagon off him and then he laughed. "It's lucky I have two feet."

And, Francis found, they ate like wolves. He

hunted to feed them and it took three full deer or one small buffalo a *day,* eating three times a day. He'd never seen such appetites and he could remember Grimes sitting down and eating ten pounds of meat in one sitting at one meal.

Lottie changed her mind about doing women's work and cooked for them—though the men washed and cleaned up after she was done—and ten days into their journey together she sighed, looking at the empty pots. "I cook more each time and they eat it all. I don't think I could cook enough to fill them."

It would have been easy to consider them friends. Francis and Lottie and Billy traveled with the men and laughed with them and were close to them, but Francis and Lottie and Billy had the problem of the gold they'd earned. Billy hunted with Francis, using his bow to take turkeys, rabbits and squirrels for what the men called "bites now and again," and that left Lottie alone with the Spanish gold.

What they had amounted to a fortune. Though Francis had not worked it out—sums bored him and for the moment it didn't matter anyway, since there was no place to spend it— the amount was enough to cause greed and desire. So Francis and Lottie and Billy had kept the gold hidden, wrapped in private packs rolled in green hide in back of one of the wagons in a space that the men had provided. But the gold came between them and the men, for it was a secret to be kept, and the more Francis came to like the men, the less he liked the feeling of not being honest.

They had traveled for two weeks. Francis, Lottie and Billy had fallen into the routine of hunting, traveling, cooking and eating, helping with the wagons if it was needed, which it almost never was, and moving slowly through the country.

They covered ground at a snail's pace, rarely making more than ten miles a day, and it often frustrated Francis, who was used to the freedom and relative speed of horseback travel.

"When we get up," Billy whined one morning, "we can see where we're going to sleep tonight."

"It makes no never mind," Lottie said to him, slapping him across the back of his head—though much more lightly than she formerly had. "The company is good and we're moving in the right direction."

In two weeks they had come not much more than a hundred and twenty miles but the country had changed dramatically. They had gone through a small range of mountains, working down several passes that were fairly easy going and came out in some break country that was semidesert. From a distance, it looked almost flat but as they approached it the country turned into a nightmare. The smoothness gave way to steep-sided gullies and ditches that made wagon travel almost impossible. The wagons hung up, tee-tered, fell, crashed down, half rolled over and were jerked to the next gully. Francis and Billy were off a long time hunting. Game had become more scarce as they left the mountains and they had to work harder for meat, and by the time they came back to the camp with two deer and half a dozen rabbits the men had a fire going and were settled into doing camp chores, mending broken wagons, torn harness and the like. But tonight there was a difference; something had changed. They seemed reserved, not talkative—even Billy and Lottie noticed it—and Francis could not see the reason.

He shrugged it off at first, sat by a fire to sharpen his knife, which had hit sand when he was gutting a deer and become dull. He was just finishing it up when Orson came to him.

"Francis," Orson said in his deep, even voice. "We must talk."

Francis looked up. "All right. Let's talk."

"Over there, by John's wagon, where we can be alone."

The hairs went up on Francis's neck and he stood and hefted his rifle, slid his knife back in its sheath. "Why alone?"

"Because I think you would rather be alone for what I have to say."

What on earth? Francis thought. What is he after?

Francis held back and let Orson lead so he could watch him. He liked the man and trusted him, but so much of his life had become a habit of caution, of taking care, that he couldn't help himself.

Orson stopped by John's wagon and turned, and Francis held back a step and a half. "What's wrong, Orson?"

Orson coughed, seemed embarrassed. "You have your goods in the back of John's wagon. . . ."

Francis nodded.

"We are in some hard country for wagon travel."

"I know." Francis waited.

"It is only maybe three more weeks now and we'll turn the wagons into rafts and run down the big river to the settlements. We are nearing our destination. Everybody is anxious."

Francis nodded again. He had heard them talking. They thought to make the Columbia River before long and there they would make rafts to get to the valleys where the farmers had settled.

"But now it is very hard going."

"I understand. Do you want me to stop hunting and help with the wagons? Is that what this is about?"

Orson shook his head. "No. No. It is just that the wagons break. . . . John's wagon broke and your bundle came undone."

Ah, Francis thought. There it is.

"Francis, there was so much gold there in your bundle."

"Yes. I know."

Now Orson waited and when Francis did not come forth with more information he sighed again. "We believe that a man's business is his own and I do not want to pry but the others—"

"Others? Does everybody know about the gold?"

Orson nodded. "We have no secrets. And we do not have a desire to intrude in your affairs but the others have a concern and I must confess I have some of the same feelings. Is the gold, I mean, does the gold—did you come by the gold honestly? We would not ask except that there is so very much of it."

Francis relaxed. Orson was so honest, and so obviously uncomfortable about asking . . .

"Yes. We found it." Francis quickly told him the story of discovering the grave and the Spanish armor and sword.

Orson smiled. "Such good fortune, such very good luck for you."

Francis nodded but thought again, as he had thought many times, that the gold was only good where you could spend it. And while they were closer, they were still many hard miles from where the gold would do them any good.

Chapter Ten

Francis could not believe the river.

He stood with Lottie at his right and Billy at his left, Orson and the men off to the side, and stared at the river in awe. And not a little fear.

It was half a mile across, smooth but with a fast current that made the dark waters roil so that they looked almost alive, and evil. The Columbia.

They had come across the last of the high desert plains with little further mishap and no injuries, now following a trail that was so heavily traveled it would have been impossible to get lost. They set the wagon wheels in the ruts. Game became more and more scarce and Billy and Francis ranged farther and farther afield to get meat, at times going ten or fifteen miles off the track before they found deer or elk. Buffalo had disappeared completely, hunted out in the years the wagons had been passing, as had most other game. But as they came near the river they met Indians of different bands and tribes who wanted to barter tools or steel or guns for food. The men and Francis had nothing extra to trade, but Francis, who knew the more or less universal sign language used by all the tribes to trade or talk war or peace, took some young men aside and they showed him how to catch salmon in the river, using line and bone hooks.

Francis set to fishing as soon as they reached the river. The salmon were so numerous that they seemed to fill the water, and soon he had more than enough fish for everybody. The meat was oily and thick and rich, and while it tasted fine at first, within two days Francis was ready for elk or venison again.

Work on rafts began at once. The wagons were

broken down and taken apart, huge cedar logs were cut from the surrounding forest and horses in harness were used to skid them down to the water. They lashed the logs together with rope and bark twine, and used boards from the wagons to make flooring. Then they built a pen to hold the animals.

But now the Indians, at first helpful, had changed. When it became apparent that the white men had nothing further to trade or sell, the Indians took to stealing. Any tool left lying around, a nail, a piece of rope, an auger bit, was soon gone. They hung around the camp constantly, watching the men work and waiting for a chance to grab something and run. The white men soon learned to keep track of their tools and equipment and stopped losing gear, but they began to distrust the Indians.

While fishing one day, Francis befriended a young man named Iktah. Iktah's language was almost impossible for Francis to learn because there were so many short, guttural, sharply cut-off phrases that were hard to pronounce. But they soon became almost fluid in their sign language and Francis learned to trust Iktah.

They were sitting on the bank one day just

after Francis had set his lines, watching the dark waters stream past, when Iktah pointed down the river and signed, "The water down there is not safe."

Francis signed, "Why?"

He watched Iktah carefully as he answered, "It has been a dry year. No rain, very little snow. The river will not come high as it does sometimes. It is too low. There are places where many rocks stick out of the water like sharp teeth. They will eat the boats and the men and the horses and oxen."

"Is this all true?"

"Yes."

"What must be done?"

"There is a trail back through the mountains. It will take more time but it is safe. My people could help you carry your goods and drive your animals. Do not let the men go on the river."

That night while eating—salmon, always salmon—Francis told Orson what Iktah had said.

"We have not heard of this before," Orson said. "Nobody in any group has left word."

"He says we are the first this year to try the river."

Orson shook his head. "We would have heard.

And now this man says his people will help us carry our things over the mountains? The same people who would steal us blind?"

"He says the river is too dangerous," Francis repeated. "Farther down, miles down into canyons where you cannot turn around, he says there are rocks that will tear the rafts to pieces. You cannot get through."

Orson sighed. He was not tired—Francis did not think he could ever be tired—but there was a sadness in his voice. "I think that we cannot believe what you have heard about the river. I think they merely want to steal more from us and are using this as a way to get what they want."

"Orson, I believe him. I'm going to go around."

Orson shook his head. "You have learned how to make your own way, and you must do what you think is right. We wish you well."

Francis knelt in the dirt and took a stick to sketch a map, and he thought of Grimes as he drew. How many times the mountain man had done the same thing, showing a tree, a river, mountains, drawn in the dirt as Francis did it now.

"Here we are," he said. "Iktah said it would

take seven days by horse to get back to the river below the bad places. Lottie, Billy and I will leave tomorrow with horses, and you won't be leaving for another week at least. We'll stop here, near where Iktah says there are two peaks, and camp by the river and wait. If you're right, when you come along we'll rejoin you."

"And if we're wrong . . ." Orson looked steadily at Francis.

Francis shook his head. "You'll be fine, you'll be fine."

They shook hands, and Francis went to tell Lottie and Billy to get ready. That night they packed and arranged the loads. They left at dawn, and Francis did not look at the river as they rode away. He thought only of shaking hands with Orson.

Chapter Eleven

"I don't think they're coming," Lottie said. "They decided to stay right where they were." Her eyes were hopeful as she poked the fire.

"Or maybe," Billy said, "they haven't left yet."

"Maybe." Francis nodded. "Yes, that's probably it. They haven't left yet."

But Francis didn't believe it. Orson and the other men might have delayed a day or two, but it was going on two weeks since Francis and Lottie and Billy had set out. Once they reached the river, Iktah had left them here to camp and gone back to scout. The men should have come along by now.

The three of them had been waiting for more than eight days. Billy had ranged out to hunt. Somehow he had brought down an elk with his small bow. It was a large bull—more than seven hundred pounds—and they had spent the week in a comfortable camp by the river drying elk meat and eating red meat to get the taste of salmon out of their mouths.

"Should we stop looking?" Lottie asked.

"No." Francis shook his head. They had been taking turns watching the river and standing watch by the fire at night, to keep it going so the men would see it. "Let's keep it up for a while yet."

"Maybe I should look for another elk." Billy pointed at the hills. "I saw fresh signs back about four miles. We could use the meat when they come."

"Good idea. The way they eat we'll need . . ."

Francis trailed off. It was late afternoon and he was watching the river while he spoke. The water was more than half a mile wide here but had flattened considerably and slowed down. The river was still dark, and had what must have been underwater obstacles because it seemed to boil and tumble, almost in an oily way, with thick bulges that rolled up and back under. While he watched, Francis saw the body of a man hit one of the bulges, come upright for a second with his arms up in the air, almost as if waving, and then disappear. It was too far away to tell for certain but it looked a lot like Orson. Francis nearly cried out.

While he watched, he saw the bodies of four horses and one ox float through the same eddy. Then came a large piece of wreckage that was unmistakably part of the raft Orson and the men had made from their wagons and cedar logs.

He dropped to his knees, mutely watching the water.

Then there was nothing.

Lottie and Billy had been looking away and had not seen anything but Francis felt a brush on his shoulder and turned to see Iktah standing there, making signs.

"The teeth of the river have taken your friends."

Francis nodded slowly and answered with shaking hands, "I'm afraid that is so."

"What did he say?" Lottie asked.

"He said that Orson and the rest of them aren't coming."

"Well, we can wait. I like traveling with them, even when I have to cook."

"No." Francis put his hand on her shoulder. "They aren't coming. Ever."

"Oh." Her eyes grew wide, then teared. "*Oh.* All of them?"

He nodded.

"Oh, Francis." She turned and looked at the river, across it, at the mountains behind. "Is it to be like this always? Just always so hard, so that it crushes people?" She covered her face with her hands and began to sob.

Billy had been listening silently, standing on one leg with his left foot on the inside of his right knee. And he nodded now, looking strangely weary and wise beyond his years. He looked up and down the river. "It's always been hard. I guess it always will be hard." He went up to Lottie and put his hand on her shoulder.

Francis felt less grief than a bone tiredness. He

had used up all his grief when Grimes was killed. Now he was so exhausted that even pain was dulled. He just wanted it over.

"We can't travel on the river," he said to Iktah. "Even if we had time and could do it, making the rafts would take more tools than we carry." He looked back into the mountains. "Is there a trail that will take us to what the white men call the golden valley, where the settlements begin?"

Iktah frowned, thinking. "There is talk of such a trail. It follows the river but way off to the side. I have not seen it and do not wish to go to where the white men live. But they say it is easy to follow. Just look for the dead line with the yellow flowers."

"Dead line?"

"There is no grass because the animals of the white men have eaten it all. And where the animals leave their sign in the flat places there are yellow flowers that grow tall and smell bad."

Francis had been speaking aloud, translating to Lottie and Billy as he read sign, and Lottie said, her face still wet with tears, "He means mustard, Francis. Papa showed us how the wild mustard seed is in some of the feed the wagon trains carry.

The oxen and horses eat it and it passes through them and grows where they leave their manure while they walk. We just have to follow the mustard flowers."

"How far is it?" Francis asked. "How many sleeps?"

Iktah shrugged. "Some say three, others seven or eight. It depends on how you work your horses."

Close, Francis thought. I am close to done with this. We are close to done with this. "I thank you for the time spent traveling with us."

Iktah shrugged again. "It was right to do it. Sitting by the fire with you to talk was a good time. Some things are not a good time, but this was. I will go now." And he turned his pony and disappeared. Francis waved a hand in farewell.

Then he looked at the sun. "We can make some miles before dark. You want to keep going?"

Billy was already gathering his things together. Lottie nodded. "I want to get away from this cursed river."

They broke camp quickly. Billy rode first, then Lottie, who trailed the packhorse. Francis mounted and followed them. There had been times when his life depended on water, times when he would have loved to see this river. But now he wanted shut of it. He never wanted to see it again.

—— Chapter Twelve ——

It turned out to be three days to where the settlements began. It was a quiet ride, for Francis hardly spoke, and that silenced Lottie. Francis was getting more and more anxious. Were his parents alive? How did his parents and his sister, Rebecca, look now? How would they feel when they saw him—they would have thought him dead all this time, after all. What would they think of Lottie and Billy?

If he expected to find them at once, he was to be sadly disappointed. At the first settlement they had never heard of the name Tucket, nor at the second, and in the third a man looked at them and said:

"Tucket! Now, that sounds familiar. Let me see . . ."

Lottie clutched Francis's arm.

"I got it!" the man said. "Weren't they all killed on the river?"

After that Francis nearly stopped looking.

But Lottie got her stubborn streak up. "Francis," she said, "you can't stop now. Billy and me won't let you stop."

So they rode on, Lottie talking, talking, to fill the silence.

Nine days later, in the fifth settlement, they stopped at a lean-to that served as a store and trading post. A wizened old man leaned across the board counter and said, "A family called Tucket? Would there be a girl named Rebecca?"

"Yes." Francis held his breath. How long, how many months? All the time he had spent searching now came down to this very second.

"Would she have black hair?"

"She does."

"Is it the family that lost a boy coming across, lost him to the Indians?"

"Yes!" Lottie shouted.

Francis nodded. "Lost me. They lost me."

"Ahhh." The old man nodded. "Then they must be the ones."

"Where are they? Where? Where?" Lottie could stand it no longer.

The old man looked at her, then at Francis. "Pushy little bit, ain't she?"

"Please, sir," Francis said, "where are the Tuckets?"

"The Tuckets!" Billy roared.

The old man pointed to the twin rut road that ran west from the lean-to. "Four miles that way, then one mile off the road. They have a sign with their name on it. You can't miss it."

But the three of them were already gone.

FRANCIS STOPPED HIS HORSE and sat quietly on her for a moment, watching the man in the field, letting the sight of him fill his heart. The man was plowing, working a team of horses, and he had his back to the three of them. Francis clucked to his horse and tightened his heels and the pony moved forward, walking softly but slightly faster than the plowhorses, until she was just four feet in back of the man working the plow. Lottie and Billy followed him, Billy smiling but Lottie oddly serious, with a worried look.

The man stopped and straightened his back and wiped sweat from his forehead and turned and saw what at first he took to be three Indians and a packhorse following him.

They were all dressed in buckskins, seasoned by hundreds of campfires and rain, their faces weather-blasted and burned and blackened. Francis wore his hair tied back in a club with a rawhide thong and he held a rifle that had become part of him, an extension of his arm.

"What . . . ? Who . . . ?"

Francis let him wonder for another beat. Then he slid off the horse and stood, taller than his father now, leaner, and he said, "Hello, Pa. How are you?"

For a second, then two, there was nothing. Then a look, a swift flash in the man's eyes.

"Francis?" A smile, from deep inside, and a bellow: *"Francis!"* And he reached over and jerked Francis away from the horse and was holding him and crying and hugging all at once.

And Francis was home.

Afterword

After Francis returned, his family was, of course, ecstatic. At first his mother almost could not accept it, and many times, months after he was home, she would come to his bed while he was sleeping and push his hair back from his head, kiss him on the forehead, touch his cheek. At first it bothered him. At first many things bothered him. Sleeping in the cabin his father had made was hard, since he was accustomed to sleeping outside, and having people around him all the time was hard too, and the noise of the farm. But after a time he came to like the closeness, the hard work, the wonderful food made of so many things besides meat. The wonderful food made by his mother and Rebecca.

He liked farming, working alongside his father, the way his father said "son." He liked going for walks with Rebecca, and how she made him laugh. He liked the way Rebecca, Lottie and Billy became good friends.

Lottie and Billy stayed briefly with the Tuckets, then were taken in by another family who had lost their children to cholera on the way across. They lived just over a hill and saw the Tuckets nearly every day.

After they all got settled, there was the question of the Spanish treasure. Francis and Lottie and Billy were almost staggeringly rich, for they had seventy-five pounds of gold and sixty pounds of silver among the three of them. The gold alone was so valuable that the same amount would have made them multimillionaires in modern times.

It's hard to get exact ratios, but it must be remembered that the main reason the Oregon Trail existed, and that such a huge percentage of the population went west (the largest mass migration in American history) was that hundreds of banks were failing and the country was in a severe depression. People had lost farms, houses, land. Nearly everybody was dirt poor—literally.

And this poverty was most extreme in the new West. Everything was done by barter or trade. Money, in the form of currency, hardly existed, and anybody who had money, or gold and silver, was in a very good position to make more.

At the tender age of eleven Lottie became something of a banker. And Francis was glad to leave her in charge. Billy was too. Once he'd bought and eaten his fill of rock candy, the money didn't interest Billy. So Lottie loaned the money at interest, investing and reinvesting, so that in three short years she had nearly doubled the amount they'd found in the Spanish grave. Through defaults in loans she acquired two farms and a sawmill, which she leased back to the previous owners and continued to earn money on.

Meanwhile, Francis worked with his father on the farm. For a time he was content with the work and life as it was.

Then there came a day when he went to see Lottie about something financial and he wasn't sure why, but on the way he stopped and picked some wildflowers and handed them to her when he arrived. And she nodded and smiled in a soft new way and put them in a jar with water.

The next day he brought flowers again. She

smiled. And so, gradually, Francis and Lottie changed the way they thought about each other.

Almost one year later to the day, they wed. The day after the marriage, Billy ran off to sea.

"I want to see more of the world," he said. "I'll be back."

And he did come back. But in the meantime Francis and Lottie set up housekeeping on a farm down the road. Four years later Billy returned. The three of them now owned many farms, several large herds of brood mares and horses, a wagon factory, four sawmills, three small hotels. Billy took some of his money and bought a square-rigged sailing ship and started a shipping line. Within five years he had three more ships and was hauling wood, cut by his own sawmills, to China to trade for tea and porcelain, which he shipped east to Europe, and then brought people back from Europe to the East Coast before starting the circle again.

When he could, Billy returned home. He also married and had children, and Lottie and Francis had children, who in turn married and had children, and much of the states of Oregon and Washington are owned by their children and their children's children and *their* children.

Francis lived to be an old man and died in 1923. Lottie lived seven years longer. They never traveled again. They lived their lives in a small frame house just over the hill from the original Tucket homestead, amassing one of the great American fortunes. Each evening, after supper, Francis would take his rifle and go sit among the trees as the sun went down and think of prairies and storms and Indians and mountain men and herds of buffalo and grizzlies and horizons—oh yes, horizons—and every night the last thought before he went back to the house to drink a cup of warm tea and to sleep, every night he'd think the same thought of a one-armed mountain man leaning back against a tree, dead.

Every night his last thought was of Jason Grimes.

─── Author's Note ───

When we think of the American West, most of us think in images and ideas that come from the time of the cowboys. Countless books (some of them mine), plays, songs, radio programs, television shows and movies have been devoted to it. Actually that period lasted only thirty years or so, from the end of the Civil War in 1865 until about 1895. Yet it often seems that more energy has been devoted to this brief time than to all the history preceding it.

Of course, what we know as the American West is a place that existed long before human beings appeared on Earth. The mountains we see today have been relatively unchanged for millions of years. In prehistoric times, the Western states were a swampy jungle filled with enormous reptiles, dinosaurs and other creatures now long extinct. At another time huge stretches of the West were ocean bottom, a place where sharks as big as buses hunted and killed.

Most of the period since humans first appeared in the West (approximately 28,000 B.C.) is unrecorded. Archaeological discoveries show that people have lived in Western canyons, deserts and mountains perhaps more than twenty thousand years. While much is made of how "new" America is compared to Europe, Native American culture predates much of European culture. Early inhabitants are still a powerful presence in the West today. In my own travels, I've come across thousands of pictographs—ancient paintings and drawings on rock walls—that were created centuries before Christopher Columbus began his voyage to the New World from Spain in 1492. I've seen pictographs that are personal narratives showing people gutting animals after a hunt, or a figure shooting arrows at other figures to frighten them away from his crops—stories of achievement and also, perhaps, a warning to enemies.

Long before the explorers Lewis and Clark made their great expedition from St. Louis to the

Pacific between 1804 and 1806, and still longer before Francis Tucket made his journey, the West was not wild but largely civilized and tamed. Native Americans had lived there successfully for thousands of years. After the Spanish conquest in the 1540s, Spanish soldiers began to explore the West, and Catholic missionaries started to establish a system of missions and churches, many of which are still in use today. The Spanish founded Santa Fe about 1610, San Antonio in 1718, San Diego in 1769 and Los Angeles in 1781. San Francisco was founded in 1776, the year the thirteen colonies declared America's independence from England.

In that same year men left to map a trade route from Santa Fe in New Mexico to Monterey in California to make it easier to transport goods to the coast. A traveler going south from Santa Fe into Mexico would find small inns, forerunners of our motels, at intervals where he could rest his horses and pack mules. These inns were known as *fondas,* a word still in use today.

But to the north there were still vast tracts of wilderness inhabited by Native Americans and a very few mountain men and French trappers. This is where I brought Francis, because I wanted to write about an area and a time largely neglected in history books and ignored by movies and television.

It was a time of great adventure, when you could ride through herds of buffalo for days and when mountain ranges bounded on forever, when everything was new and raw and savage and when Francis was limited only by himself—and by nature.

Some readers have commented on the violence and hardship of Francis's life, the amount of fighting and death and difficulty. Nothing in these books about Francis Tucket is completely fictional—every act of violence, every difficulty is based on reality and actually happened to some person who existed then. This includes the attacks by the Comancheros, the skirmishes following the Mexican War and the scavengers who deserted from the army and roamed and pillaged. The hardships that people faced trying to go west by wagon, on foot or on horseback were staggering. Several people died for every mile covered on the so-called Oregon Trail. They died from cholera, typhus, typhoid fever, gun accidents, simple flu, ear infections, rabies, infections from small cuts, blood poisoning, scurvy and other malnutritional diseases; they died from attacks by bands of robbers, from being run over by wagons, from drowning, from botulism and other food poisoning and from simple childhood diseases like measles and chicken pox.

They did not, however, die in attacks by Native Americans, which is the way Hollywood tells it. In the time of the Oregon Trail the Native Americans were helpful, often providing food and guidance, and there was rarely, very rarely, an attack on a wagon train, and never a time when the settlers had to "circle the wagons" and fight. That happened only in the movies. All the difficulty with Native Americans came later, after they were invaded by the military and their lands were stolen. This happened after 1860, by which time there was a railroad across the continent and the Oregon Trail was a thing of the past.

Don't miss any of the books in the TUCKET ADVENTURES!

Share the excitement of Francis Tucket's travels as he heads west on the Oregon Trail.

"Many readers will love these books for their exciting, nonstop action." —*School Library Journal*

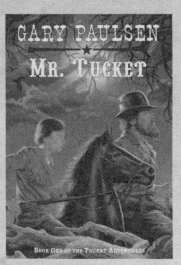

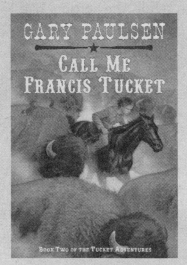

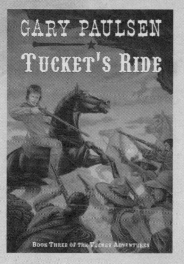

GARY PAULSEN

TUCKET'S RIDE

BOOK THREE OF THE TUCKET ADVENTURES

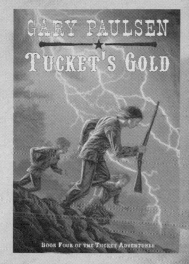

GARY PAULSEN

TUCKET'S GOLD

BOOK FOUR OF THE TUCKET ADVENTURES

GARY PAULSEN

TUCKET'S HOME

BOOK FIVE OF THE TUCKET ADVENTURES

BOOK ONE

Mr. Tucket

Fourteen-year-old Francis Tucket is heading west on the Oregon Trail with his family by wagon train. When he receives a rifle for his birthday, he's thrilled to be treated like an adult. But Francis lags behind to practice shooting and is captured by Pawnees. It will take wild horses, hostile tribes and a mysterious one-armed mountain man named Mr. Grimes to help Francis become the man who will be called Mr. Tucket.

BOOK TWO

Call Me Francis Tucket

Alone. Now that Francis and Mr. Grimes, the mountain man, have parted ways, Francis is heading west on his Indian pony, trying to find his family. After months with Mr. Grimes, Francis has learned to live by the harsh code of the wilderness. He can cause a stampede, survive his own mistakes and face up to desperadoes. But when he rescues a little girl and her younger brother, Francis takes on more than he bargained for.

BOOK THREE

Tucket's Ride

When winter comes early to the prairie, Francis, Lottie and Billy turn south to avoid the cold and ride right into enemy territory, into the aftermath of the Mexican War. They're captured by the dreaded Comancheros, the most ruthless outlaws Francis has ever seen. The Comancheros take them away—away from the trail west, away from civilization and away from any chance of rescue.

BOOK FOUR
Tucket's Gold

Things look grim for Francis, Lottie and Billy. Without water, horses or food, they're alone in a prairie wasteland with the Comanchero outlaws in pursuit. Enemies new and old wait at every turn, and death might strike at any moment. But so might good fortune. When they stumble on an ancient treasure, they must use teamwork, courage and fast thinking to hold on to it.